This book is dedicated to the children of the brave men and women
of the United States military, who have risked their lives to keep America safe.
Thank you for your service to our nation.
—J. B.

To all military families
—R. C.

Endpaper art created by Natalie Biden

ACKNOWLEDGMENTS

There are many people whose efforts made this book possible. Special thanks to the incredible team at Simon & Schuster for both their support of this story and their tireless work, especially Carolyn Reidy, Jon Anderson, Paula Wiseman, and Paul Crichton. Thanks also to Raúl Colón, Bob Barnett, Deneen Howell, Robert Burleigh, and Courtney O'Donnell for their dedication and passion. I appreciate all the people who shared their stories and offered their expertise, and of course I am grateful to Natalie, Hunter, Hallie, and Beau for inspiring this project and making me a proud military mom and nana. —J. B.

SIMON & SCHUSTER BOOKS FOR YOUNG READERS • An imprint of Simon & Schuster Children's Publishing Division • 1230 Avenue of the Americas, New York, New York 10020 • Text copyright © 2012 by Jill Biden • Illustrations copyright © 2012 by Raúl Colón • All rights reserved, including the right of reproduction in whole or in part in any form. • SIMON & SCHUSTER BOOKS FOR YOUNG READERS is a trademark of Simon & Schuster, Inc. • For information about special discounts for bulk purchases, please contact Simon & Schuster Special Sales at 1-866-506-1949 or business@simonandschuster.com. • The Simon & Schuster Speakers Bureau can bring authors to your live event. For more information or to book an event, contact the Simon & Schuster Speakers Bureau at 1-866-248-3049 or visit our website at www.simonspeakers.com. • Book design by Lizzy Bromley • The text for this book is set in Granjon. • The illustrations for this book are rendered in watercolor, colored pencil, and lithograph pencil. • Manufactured in the United States of America • 0412 LAK • 10 9 8 7 6 5 4 3 2 1 • Library of Congress Cataloging-in-Publication Data • Biden, Jill. • Don't forget, God bless our troops / Jill Biden ; illustrated by Raúl Colón. • p. cm. • Includes bibliographical references. • Audience: Grades K-3. • ISBN 978-1-4424-5735-5 (hbk. : alk. paper) 1. Children of military personnel—United States—Juvenile literature. 2. Families of military personnel—United States—Juvenile literature. 3. Soldiers—Family relationships—United States—Juvenile literature. 4. Children of military personnel—United States. 5. Families of military personnel—United States. I. Colón, Raúl ill. II. Title. • UB403.B55 2012 • 355.1'20973—dc23 • 2012008493 • ISBN 978-1-4424-5737-9 (eBook)

first edition

Don't Forget, God Bless Our Troops

JILL BIDEN
Illustrated by RAÚL COLÓN

SIMON & SCHUSTER BOOKS FOR YOUNG READERS
New York London Toronto Sydney New Delhi

Letter from the Author

Dear Reader,

It is my wish that this book will make all Americans, especially children, aware of the experiences of children who have a mom or dad deployed in our armed forces. This story is based on my family, but it represents the experiences of thousands of military families all across this country. Only 1 percent of Americans are serving in the military, but their families serve too, and all Americans need to be aware of the sacrifices military families are making for the safety of all of us.

My experience through my son's deployment made me realize how important it is for all Americans to get a glimpse inside the life of a military family and to understand what it means when a family member is deployed. I hope Natalie's story gives readers some insight and encourages them to commit a simple act of kindness toward a military family.

God bless our troops,

Jill Biden

At the deployment ceremony for my son, the general's wife quietly slipped a prayer into my hand. I hope it will offer comfort and hope for others as it did for me:

I pray to give each soldier the courage and the strength to do the duty that is required of them. May they always remember our appreciation for the sacrifice they and their families are making for us. We are thankful for the men and women who are willing to risk their lives to protect our freedom. Please go with each one of them and protect them wherever they go.

"DOES DADDY REALLY HAVE TO GO?"

"Daddy is a soldier," Natalie's mom answers
in a quiet voice. "Soldiers have to do hard things
sometimes." She runs her hand through Natalie's hair.

Her father takes Natalie in his arms. "Home is
wherever I'm with you!" he sings softly.

Natalie smiles. "I like that song, Daddy. I like it,"
she whispers.

Natalie sits on the floor of her room with stuffed animals around her.

Her dolls are here. Her books are here. Even her dog, Webbie, is here.

But one thing isn't here. Daddy isn't here.

Outside, the October sky is gray. Leaves are falling.
Daddy's not here, Natalie thinks again, as she watches
a red leaf drift past the window and out of sight.

Natalie calls it "The day we eat turkey!"

"Make a wish," says Nana, "and pull!"

Tug! *Snap!*

Natalie pulls the wishbone and wins.

"I wish that Daddy would . . ."

"Shhh," Nana says, putting a finger to her lips. "Keep your wish secret, and hope that someday it will come true."

Be brave, Natalie.

The wind is blowing outside the kitchen window.
Natalie helps her mother bake holiday cookies.
"Yum!" says her little brother, Hunter. They will send
the cookies to Daddy.
"Will Daddy be coming home?" Natalie suddenly asks.
Natalie sees her mother turn away and wipe her eyes.
She runs over and puts her arms around her mom.
"I love you, Mommy. I love you."
Be brave, Natalie.

So many people are kind to the family.

Yesterday the neighbors brought over a homemade pizza.

Today Dad's friend Alex is shoveling the sidewalk.

"Your dad is sure helping our country," Alex says. "I want to help too!"

On the lawn Natalie and Hunter are rolling big snowballs! They are making a snowman.

Natalie puts an army cap on the snowman's head.

Hunter claps his hands and cheers. "Yeah!"

"A snow soldier!" Natalie shouts.

Be brave, Natalie.

Natalie stands in the church hallway, looking at a page of the church bulletin.

She touches the page. *Here.*

Her father's name is here, along with the names of many other soldiers.

People will pray for all of them. A girl behind her is also looking at the names.

Natalie wonders, *Is* her *daddy or mommy far from home too? Is her mommy or daddy safe?*

"Hi," Natalie says shyly.

"Hi," the girl answers, smiling.

Right away Natalie knows they will become friends.

Be brave, Natalie.

Natalie's baby tooth is hanging by a thread.

Mom turns on the computer and gets Dad on video chat.

"Daddy, Daddy!" Hunter waves.

"Natalie's tooth is ready to come out," says Mom. "She's going to pull it."

Natalie sees her dad waving and waves back.

"I'm afraid, Daddy! It may hurt."

Dad smiles. "Go, go, go! You're a big girl!"

Natalie's teacher holds up a picture.

There are many soldiers in the picture, and one of them is Natalie's dad.

The teacher points to him. "The soldiers are far, far away," she says. "They are fighting for our country."

Natalie feels special. Proud.

On her way to recess she looks at the picture again. She leans over and kisses her dad right on the nose.

Be brave, Natalie.

Natalie and Hunter are playing soldier with
their Daddy Dolls.

Hunter starts to cry. "I want Daddy!"

Natalie holds her doll up in front of her face. She
pretends the doll is a puppet. "Don't cry, Hunter!
Be a big, strong boy," she says in a daddy voice.

"That's not Daddy talking!" says Hunter.

"Yes it is. That's what Daddy would say."

Hunter nods. He stops crying. He wipes his eyes.

Be brave, Natalie.

"Ooooh, I'm tired." Natalie yawns.

Natalie and Hunter are staying overnight at Nana and Pop's house. Hunter is already asleep. Natalie snuggles next to her grandmother.

"We had a busy day, didn't we, Nana?"

Nana smiles. "But it was a good day. You were such a helper, too! We sent hundreds of boxes overseas. You know, honey, your daddy isn't the only soldier in the army. There are many soldiers far away from home along with him! Now they'll know we care! Okay, let's say prayers before you fall asleep."

Natalie closes her eyes and everything is quiet. Then she opens her eyes for a brief moment.

"And don't forget, Nana," she says in a sleepy voice, "God bless our troops."

Be brave, Natalie.

Natalie stares down at the blue, shimmering water. She hears the sounds of splashing kids.

"I can't, Mommy!"

Her mother stands in the pool, waving. "You can do it! Pretend you're swimming to Daddy!"

Natalie takes a deep breath. "One, two, three, jump!"

Natalie feels the water over her head. She sputters as she comes up laughing.

"I did it, Mommy. I did it, I did it!"

Be brave, Natalie.

Natalie and Hunter wear their army T-shirts all summer.

Their mom chuckles. "Natalie, that shirt is so dirty it can stand up by itself! Let me wash it!"

"But, Mommy, soldiers get dirty when they wear their uniforms. Why can't I?"

Webbie seems to agree.

"Woof, woof!" Webbie barks. "Woof, woof!"

Natalie is making a picture.

Carefully she draws long red stripes, leaving white spaces after each one. Next she picks up a crayon and colors in a blue square in the corner. Then she dots the blue square with white stars.

It has to be the best picture ever. It's for someone very special!

Be brave, Natalie.

Natalie is so excited! She bounces here. She bounces there.
She sees soldiers everywhere hugging their families.
Suddenly she sees someone hurrying toward them.
"Mommy, Hunter, Nana, everyone—there's Daddy!"
Natalie races to her father and hugs him around the legs.

He lifts her up, up, up to his shoulders.
"Daddy, my brave Daddy!"
Her dad laughs.
"No, no, no—it's you, my little Natalie!
You are my brave, brave girl!"

Author's Note

Our military families are strong, proud, and resilient. But their service comes with challenges and sacrifices. Many military families have to move several times during their years of service. This means that children frequently change schools and are separated from friends and activities, spouses transition to new communities and jobs, and a mom or dad may take on the responsibility of two parents while the other is away. All these families feel a strong sense of pride and patriotism—but there is always an underlying sense of worry until their loved ones return home safely.

Through my experience of having my son deployed to Iraq for a year, I saw the impact of that deployment on my own two grandchildren, Natalie and Hunter. Our community embraced us with love and support—the thoughtful acts of kindness meant so much to all of us. For example, our church listed my son Beau's name in the bulletin every Sunday. I can't tell you how much it meant when people told me that they were praying for my son. When I least expected it, complete strangers would come up to me to thank me for my son's service. Friends sent cards and notes, all of which were uplifting and thoughtful.

The holidays were especially hard. Our family would try hard to act as though everything was normal. Beau's absence during Christmas, Thanksgiving, and birthdays was always heartbreaking, especially for his children.

First Lady Michelle Obama and I formed Joining Forces—an effort to make all Americans aware of what these families endure and to encourage them to support our troops and families as they support us. As Second Lady and a military mom, I have traveled the United States and around the world meeting thousands of military families. I have visited hundreds of wounded warriors at hospitals, burn centers, and rehabilitation facilities. These men and women have shown amazing courage and inspiring optimism. I am in awe of the resilience and strength of these military families. For many of them, their injuries have changed their lives forever, altering dreams and careers. Yet not one complains. They are ordinary Americans who have done extraordinary things.

About Our Military

America's military service members represent only 1 percent of the American population, but they carry the responsibility of protecting our entire nation. More than 2.2 million service members proudly serve in America's all-volunteer force in the active, National Guard, and Reserve components. And as this book demonstrates, when our troops are called to serve, so too are their families. Military families make incredible sacrifices, missing birthdays, anniversaries, graduations, and so many of the daily moments we spend with the people we love.

There are 1.9 million children, from newborn to eighteen years old, who are the sons and daughters of our military—1.3 million of whom are school-age. Every day these extraordinary young people shoulder responsibilities and worries that make them wise beyond their years. These brave boys and girls watch their parents go to work wearing our nation's uniform. They may have had or will have one or even both parents deployed overseas and standing in harm's way. They may have to care for a parent who is wounded or, in the most painful situations, be called to keep alive the memory of a fallen hero whom they called Mom or Dad.

In their steadfast support of those in harm's way coupled with their dedication to America, military families show us what words like "service," "strength," and "sacrifice" really mean.

How You Can Help

Only 37 percent of our military families live on military installations or bases; the majority live in more than four thousand communities nationwide. Members of our National Guard and Reserve and their families can face particular challenges because they may live outside military communities, where neighbors or colleagues do not know that they are serving. Members of our National Guard and Reserve and their families are our friends and neighbors, our teachers and small business owners; they drop everything and report to duty when called.

All Americans can find ways to recognize and support the military and military families in their own communities. Your actions can be as simple as reaching out to the new military family in your neighborhood or connecting with one of the many organizations dedicated to supporting our service members and their families. There is a role for each and every one of us in supporting military families and particularly military children.

If you live near a military base, contact the base's Family Resource Center for ways to get involved.

Every state has a National Guard unit, and you can reach out to the Family Readiness Group in your state to find out how you can get involved. Many business places, churches, synagogues, other religious institutions, and other groups organize outreach and volunteer opportunities.

Below are some national organizations that provide information about military families or opportunities for volunteers across the country:

✭ **Joining Forces: joiningforces.gov**

Joining Forces is a White House initiative aimed at encouraging all Americans to support troops and their families. The website provides ways for citizens to connect directly with volunteer opportunities in communities across the country.

✭ **USO: uso.org**

The USO (United Service Organizations) provides morale, welfare and recreational services, and support to members of the US military and their families through hundreds of their centers and events around the world.

✭ **American Red Cross: redcross.org**

The American Red Cross has a long history of providing services to members of America's military and their families during conflicts, peacekeeping, and humanitarian operations.

✭ **Blue Star Families: bluestarfam.org**

Blue Star Families aims to raise awareness among civilians of the challenges of military life. The organization was formed in December of 2008 by a group of military spouses, and now includes spouses and families from all services, veterans, and civilians.

✭ **National Military Family Association: militaryfamily.org**

The National Military Family Association is dedicated to strengthening quality of life for military families, and provides a number of resources for families and communities.

How to Reach Out to Military Children in Your Community

Tips for kids!

★ Make military kids and teens feel welcome when they move to your neighborhood—invite them to participate in your sports activities, scouts, or other clubs.

★ Listen to the concerns and discuss the worries of military friends.

★ Don't just thank the military parent for their service to our country, thank the whole family.

★ Volunteer with a military charity.

★ Remember, military children are kids just like you—when in doubt, treat them as you would want to be treated.

★ Offer to be a buddy to new military children who have recently enrolled in your school. You can help them navigate the new school, sit with them at lunch, and make sure they have people to sit with at school and after-school events.

★ Invite children of military families to go with you to sports games at your school, drama activities, dances, and parties. Pick them to be on your team.

★ Military children have often moved schools or places nine or more times. They may have been in really interesting parts of the United States and the world. Some have lived in Europe, Asia, the Middle East, or all over our country. Take the time to find out where else they have lived and ask them about any cool stories they have from living in other countries and cultures.

★ When a military child moves away, help to prepare a special gift for the student to take with him or her. Ideas might include a memory book with photos and notes from classmates, a school T-shirt signed by classmates, a framed photo, or even a stuffed animal that is the mascot of the school.

★ Sometimes military children miss days of school because a parent is leaving on or returning from a mission—called a deployment. Offer to be a part of a study group before tests, keep them informed of assignments, or bring them their homework when they've been absent.

★ Sometimes military children come from different states or countries whose schools have not covered the same class material that your school has. If you see that they are behind in an area, ask if you can help. They might have covered material that your school has not done yet, and they can help you, too.

★ Military children may be worried about a parent who is in a dangerous area. Don't be afraid to just be a good friend. Offering support and understanding is the most important thing you can do for a friend. If they are worried about a parent or family member, you can listen and be there for them.

What schools and community groups can do to support military children:

Celebrating the efforts of military families as a class or school is a great way to make kids from military families feel welcome. Here are some ideas you can suggest to your teacher, principal, or other community group leader.

✷ Plant a garden or a tree: Gardens are often used to learn about healthy eating habits, but they can also be used to honor local heroes, such as members of the military. Special plaques, flags, or markers can be planted in the soil as reminders of military parents' or community members' military service.

✷ Make a bulletin board: A map of the United States—or of the world—on a wall of the classroom can be used to show places where your classroom friends, both military and civilian, have lived.

✷ Create a hero wall: Students in your class and other friends can bring in photos of their heroes or make small posters about someone in their family who has served in the military. These can be parents who are currently serving in the military or family members who served long ago. Some classes and groups have interviewed family members to find out about the person's job in the military or if they served in a war.

✷ If a parent or family member of a student in the classroom is deployed—and the student doesn't mind discussing it— find out where the family member is going and do some research about the culture the military parent will experience while he or she is there.

✷ Send letters or cards to deployed service members.

✷ Ask your teachers or principal to have school-wide celebrations or ceremonies around military holidays such as Veterans Day, Memorial Day, service birthdays, Pearl Harbor Day, D-day, and other national days on which the sacrifices of military families are publicly honored.

The author wishes to thank the National Military Family Association and Ron Avi Astor and Linda Jacobson (USC Building Capacity in Military-Connected Schools Consortium) for their contributions to these resources. All military-related statistics were sourced from the US Department of Defense Demographics 2010: Profile of the Military Community Report.

Additional toolkits and resources for military children and families:

Military kids toolkit: militaryfamily.org/publications/kids-toolkit

Military teen toolkit: militaryfamily.org/publications/teen-toolkit

Community toolkit: militaryfamily.org/publications/community-toolkit